HAPPY BIRTHDAY
AMELIA

THIS BOOK BELONGS TO:

_____

HAPPY BIRTHDAY AMELIA

NICOLA MOON

Illustrated by Jenny Jones

PAVILION

For Imogen

First published in Great Britain in 1999 by
PAVILION BOOKS LIMITED
London House, Great Eastern Wharf
Parkgate Road, London SW11 4NQ

This edition published 2001

Text © Nicola Moon 1999
Illustrations © Jenny Jones 1999
Design and layout © Pavilion Books Ltd. 1999

Designed by Bet Ayer

A CIP catalogue record for this book is available
from the British Library.

ISBN 1 86205 407 X

Set in Leawood
Printed in Singapore by Kyodo Printing

2 4 6 8 10 9 7 5 3 1

This book can be ordered direct from the publisher. Please contact
the Marketing Department. But try your bookshop first.

Amelia looked at the
calendar on the wall.
'It's my birthday!' she cried,
and jumped out of bed.

Her sisters,
Abigail and Anna,
were fast asleep.

Amelia ran through to her brothers' room.
Arthur and Alex were fast asleep too.
Amelia couldn't wait for her brothers and sisters
to wake up.

She ran to the top of the stairs and bumped into Grandma.
'Well I never!' said Grandma. 'What's got into you this morning,
nearly knocking your old Grandma off her feet?!'
But Amelia's head was filled
with balloons and birthday cake,
candles and cards and presents.
Her heart thumped with
excitement as she raced
down the stairs and
flung open the kitchen door.

But there weren't any
balloons.
Just Dad, ironing a
mountain of clothes,
as usual.

There wasn't a cake
with candles.
Just Mum, slicing a loaf
of bread, as usual.

There weren't any cards
or presents.
Just Angus the dog,
dozing in his basket,
as usual.

'But isn't it…?' Amelia started to speak.
'Time to collect the eggs,' said Mum, as usual.

Amelia couldn't believe it.
Surely it was meant to be her birthday?
She went back upstairs and looked at her calendar.
There it was.
All the days neatly crossed off, and a big red circle
around the number four.
It was her birthday.
It was her birthday and nobody knew.
Or everyone had forgotten.

Back down in the kitchen
Mum was making a
pot of tea, as usual.
Amelia picked up the egg
basket and went outside
with Angus.
As usual.

The sun was shining
and the air was filled with
the scent of apple blossom,
but Amelia felt too sad to notice.
Angus bounded around,
sniffing at things and
nearly got a bee up his nose,
but Amelia was too miserable
to laugh.

'It's meant to be my birthday,' she told the cats on the wall.

'They've all forgotten,' she told the ducks on the pond.

'What shall I do?' she asked old
Ebeneezer the donkey.

But the animals didn't know it
was her birthday either.
Amelia sat down by the barn
and cried.

Then she remembered Mum was waiting for the eggs.
She didn't want Mum to get cross, not on her birthday.
Amelia went into the hen house.
She loved the comforting darkness inside.
She dried her eyes and felt in the prickly straw
for the smooth, warm, new laid eggs.

At last she found one. Then two…three…four.
She put them carefully into the basket.
Then she felt something else.
Something smooth and flat.
Something made of paper – it felt like an envelope!

She went back outside.
It was an envelope!
A-m-e-l-i-a, she read.
It was for her! Someone had
remembered her birthday!
What a funny place to leave a card!
Amelia opened the envelope.

But it wasn't a birthday card inside.
It was just a picture.
A picture of the old tractor.
Amelia was puzzled.
Why would someone give her
a picture of the old tractor?
Then she had an idea.

She ran to the old tractor, and,
sure enough there was another envelope!
A-m-e-l-i-a, it said. She tore it open
as fast as she could.
This time there was a picture of the barn.

She had to hunt for ages before
she found it between two bales of hay.
A picture of Ebeneezer the donkey!
She hoped he hadn't eaten the next envelope.

Amelia got more and more excited as she hunted for
envelopes all round the farm.
Angus was getting excited too, wagging his tail and barking.
A treasure trail! Perhaps it would lead to treasure?
Or a present? Angus hoped it would lead to a rabbit.
The ducks quacked noisily on the pond as Amelia opened
yet another envelope.

'The orchard! Come on Angus!' she called.
But he was already bounding on ahead.

Amelia skipped along the track.
Behind the barn.
Past the stables.
Past the sheep in the field.

Round the corner, through the gate, into the orchard and …
Amelia stopped. She couldn't believe her eyes.
There were balloons in the trees and ribbons in the hedge.
There was a huge picnic lunch spread out on a blanket.
There was a birthday cake with candles,
and cards and presents.
There was Mum, Dad, Grandma, Abigail, Anna,
Arthur and Alex.

'HAPPY BIRTHDAY AMELIA!'

they shouted.

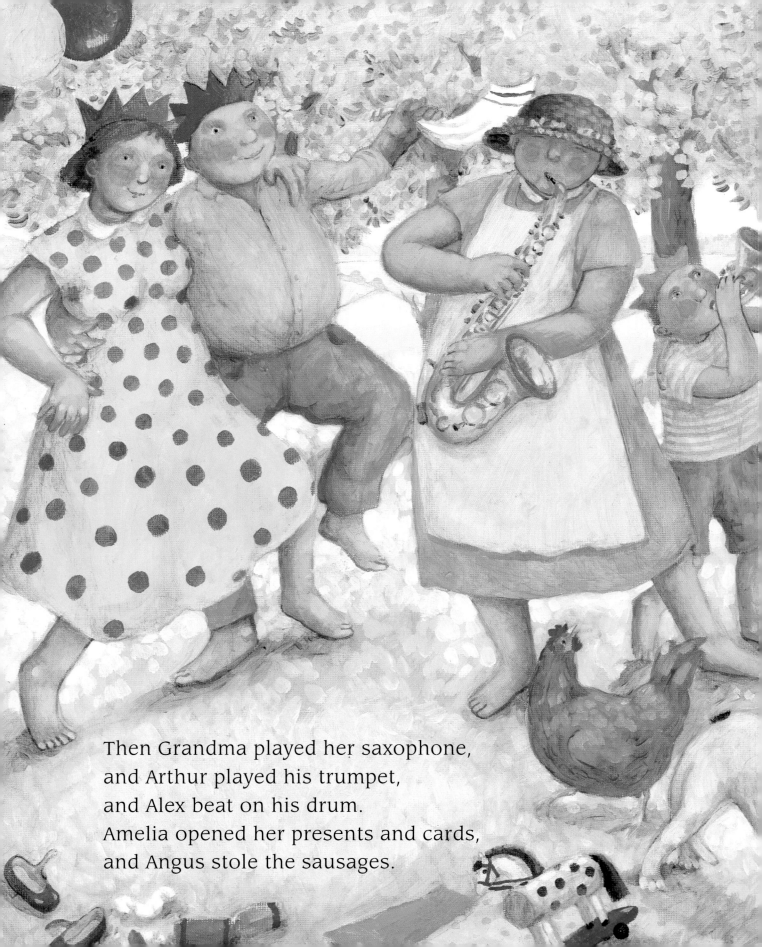

Then Grandma played her saxophone,
and Arthur played his trumpet,
and Alex beat on his drum.
Amelia opened her presents and cards,
and Angus stole the sausages.

Then they played and danced and
sang and ate and drank and played
and danced until the sun went down.
It was the best birthday
Amelia had ever had.

'Did you think we'd forgotten?' said Mum,
when Amelia was all sleepy in bed.
'Not really,' said Amelia.
Mum gave Amelia a great big hug.
'We would never forget,' she said.
'Not ever.'

Amelia snuggled down,
all warm and happy, and closed her eyes.
'Happy birthday Amelia,' said Mum.
But Amelia was fast asleep.